Hush, Little Baby

Illustrated by

Petra Brown

tiger  tales

Hush, little baby, don't say a word.

Papa's gonna buy you
a mockingbird.

And if that mockingbird
don't sing . . .

Papa's gonna buy you
a diamond ring.

And if that diamond ring
turns brass . . .

Papa's gonna buy you
a looking glass.

And if that looking glass
gets broke . . .

Papa's gonna buy you
a billy goat.

And if that billy goat
won't pull . . .

Papa's gonna buy you
a cart and bull.

And if that cart and bull
turn over . . .

Papa's gonna buy you
a dog named Rover.

And if that dog named Rover
won't bark . . .

Papa's gonna buy you
a horse and cart.

And if that horse and cart
fall down . . .

You'll still be the sweetest

little baby in town.

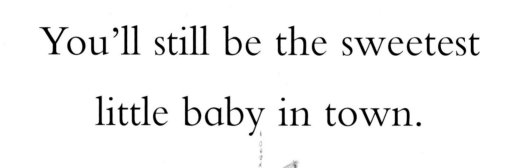

Welcome to ♥!
the Family!
Kiss Megan
Bera